CONTENTS

Chapter 1

The Band – and the Baby

Mark loved music. Most of all, he loved playing his guitar. He and his three best friends had a band called Vampire Jam and they played together every week. Jakob was the singer, Emma was on keyboard and Nell was the drummer.

Every Saturday they met in Nell's garage and played for three hours solid – with a hot chocolate break at half time. It was fantastic. Mark never, ever missed a practice at Nell's on Saturday morning.

Until the Saturday his baby sister was born.

She was born a week early, at two o'clock in the morning. When Mark and his big sister Janet woke up, Granny was in the kitchen, getting their breakfast.

"Your mum and dad went off to hospital while you were asleep," Granny said. "And now you've got a new little sister. We'll go and see her as soon as we've finished breakfast."

"Yay!" Janet said. She loved babies.

Mark was excited too. But – it was Saturday morning. "What about the band?" he said. "We always practise on Saturdays."

Granny smiled. "A baby sister is more important than band practice," she said. "You'll have to miss it this morning."

Mark texted Nell.

**Can't come this morning. Going to see
our new baby.**

Great! Nell texted back. **Lucky you!!**

Mark groaned. Nell had heaps of little
cousins and she loved babies even more than
Janet did.

As soon as they'd eaten their toast and
cornflakes, Granny drove Mark and Janet to
the hospital. They went to the Birth Centre
and found Mum and Dad sitting by a little cot,
gazing down at the baby.

"Isn't she gorgeous?" Mum said. "We're
going to call her Amber."

Mark looked at his baby sister. 'Hmm,' he
thought. 'Gorgeous?' She was small and pink,
with red hair and a funny little face. She was
fast asleep.

"Oh, she's *sweet!*" Janet said. She bent over and gave the baby a kiss.

That was a BIG BAD mistake. The baby's eyes fluttered open, she looked up at Janet's smiling face and she started to scream.

"Don't cry, Baby Amber," Mum said. "Your big sister just gave you a kiss. Ssshhh." She lifted the baby out of the cot and cuddled her. But the "ssshhh" and the cuddles didn't work. Baby Amber screamed even louder.

"Never mind," Dad said. "She'll be fine when we get her home."

But he was wrong. When they got home, Baby Amber screamed even more. She screamed so hard her little face scrunched up and turned purple. Mum tried feeding her. Dad tried rocking her. Granny tried stroking the top of her head. Nothing did any good.

Amber's screams went on and on and ON.

"It's all my fault," Janet wailed. "I shouldn't have kissed her." She started to cry too.

Mum hugged Janet. Dad rocked the baby again. And the screaming got louder and louder and LOUDER. It was so loud it hurt

Mark's ears. He couldn't bear the noise any more.

He went and fetched his guitar. "Is it OK if I go to Nell's now?" he said. "For the end of band practice?"

Dad looked round and nodded. "Yes, it's fine. Just be back in time for lunch."

So Mark put his guitar in its case and went off to Nell's garage.

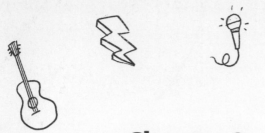

Chapter 2

Trouble in the Band

When Mark got there, Nell was in the garage, all on her own. She looked cross. She was sitting in front of her drum kit, but she wasn't playing. She had a fierce scowl on her face and she was tapping the drum sticks on her hand.

"What's up?" Mark said. "Where are the others?"

Nell pulled a face. "Emma said the band was rubbish without you. That made Jakob angry, so he shouted at her. Emma shouted back. And then they both stormed off home."

"Well, they'd better get over it," Mark said. "I'm here now."

"That's good," Nell said. "But what about your new baby?"

Mark shook his head. "She's OK," he said. "But she screams ALL the time and it makes my ears hurt. So Dad said I could come to band practice. Can we get the others back here?"

Nell picked up her phone. "I'll text them," she said.

Ten minutes later Emma and Jakob were there. Jakob was still sulking and Emma scowled when she saw him, but they said they were ready to practise.

They played a couple of slow songs and then crashed into 'Not Monday AGAIN!'. That was fast and loud and Nell went wild on the drums. By the end, everyone was smiling.

"That was brilliant," Mark said. "We're playing really well together."

"Thank goodness for that," Emma said. "Because – guess what? I've got us a gig!"

The others stared at her. "A gig?" Nell said. "What do you mean?"

Emma grinned. "We're going to be in the school show!"

"WHAT?" said Mark.

"You're joking!" said Jakob.

Emma shook her head. "No I'm not. I told Mrs Baines about our band and she asked if we'd play in the show at the end of term. So I said yes."

Jakob stared at her. "You mean – with the whole school there?" he said. "And all the parents? We're nowhere near good enough for that."

"We will be," Emma said. "If we practise enough."

"NO!" said Jakob. "We'll just make ourselves look stupid."

"I've told Mrs Baines we'll do it," Emma said. "I *promised*."

"Too bad!" Jakob shouted. "I'm not making a fool of myself in front of everyone. Vampire Jam can be in the school show if you like – but I won't be there. I'm leaving. NOW!"

And he wasn't joking. He stormed out of the garage and marched off up the road for the second time that day.

"Come back!" Nell called. "Let's talk about it."

But it was no use. Jakob had gone.

Mark glared at Emma. "That's a disaster," he said. "You've ruined everything! We can't be in the show now."

"Yes we can," Emma shouted. She folded her arms. "We're doing the show and that's all there is to it."

"But we haven't got a singer," Nell said.

"We'll find another one then," Emma yelled. "Jakob's a rubbish singer anyway. He keeps going out of tune."

"He's not rubbish," Mark said. "He's really good. You've just got cloth ears."

Emma didn't listen. She unplugged her keyboard, picked it up and stamped off with it under her arm.

Mark looked at Nell. "This is terrible," he said. "If they don't come back, the band's finished."

"Don't worry," Nell said. "Those two are always falling out. They'll get over it in a day or two."

"I hope so," said Mark. "I really hope so."

'We've got to *do* something,' Mark thought as he packed up his guitar. There must be a way to save the band. He just needed to work it out.

But when he got home, it was much too noisy to think. Baby Amber was screaming *again*.

Chapter 3

Trouble at Home

It didn't get any better. By Sunday evening,
Mark still hadn't thought of a way to save
Vampire Jam. Every time he had an idea,
Baby Amber started screaming again. He just
couldn't concentrate.

The screaming worried Granny. "I've got
my holiday in Ibiza booked for Tuesday," she
said. "But maybe I should stay here instead. To
help with the baby." She picked up Baby Amber
and tried rocking her again. "Poor little thing,
shush now," she said.

"You don't need to miss your holiday," Dad
said. "I've got two weeks off work, so I'll be
here all the time. And Mark and Janet will help
too, when they're not at school."

"What?" Granny said. She couldn't hear,
because Amber was screaming even louder.

"Don't worry about us," Mum shouted to her. "Go off and enjoy your holiday in the sun. Everything's fine."

So Granny flew to Ibiza on Tuesday.

But everything wasn't fine. Monday was horrible and Tuesday was even worse. On Tuesday evening, Mum took Baby Amber to the doctor.

"Don't worry," the doctor said. "There's nothing wrong with her. Just a bit of colic."

Mark didn't know what colic was. But he knew it made Baby Amber scream. The whole house was full of noise, noise, NOISE.

And school was just as bad. Emma and Jakob were always shouting at each other.

"If we're not in the school show, I'm leaving Vampire Jam!" Emma kept yelling.

"If we ARE in the show, then I'm leaving Vampire Jam!" Jakob kept shouting back.

Mark wanted to try and sort things out, but Nell wouldn't let him.

"It's better to leave them alone," she said. "They'll cool down in the end."

But they didn't cool down. Not one bit. When school ended on Wednesday, they were still shouting at each other as they stamped out of the playground. Mark trailed home in misery, dragging his feet and worrying about the band.

'Things can't get any worse!' he thought in despair.

But he was wrong.

On Thursday morning, while they were having a very noisy breakfast, Mum's phone rang. She picked it up. "Hello?" And then she gasped. "Oh no! That's *terrible!*"

It was a phone call from Ibiza. Granny had slipped and fallen at the hotel swimming pool. She'd broken her leg.

"I'll have to fly out and make sure she's OK," Dad said. "Can you manage without me?"

"Of course," Mum said. "I'll have Mark and Janet to help me."

Janet nodded. "I can look after Baby Amber when I get back from school. Then you can get some sleep, Mum."

Mark nodded. "And I'll do the shopping."

"Brilliant!" Dad said. "You kids are the best." And he booked his ticket on the next flight to Ibiza.

Mark went off to school with a shopping list in his pocket. When he got there, everything was very quiet. Jakob and Emma weren't shouting any more – but that wasn't good news.

They weren't speaking to each other at all. When Jakob saw Emma, he turned his back on her. And she walked past with her nose in the air and almost bumped into him – as if he was invisible.

Mark knew they should be talking about the band, but that he couldn't bear any more shouting. His head already hurt from Amber's screaming at breakfast, and his ears needed a rest. So he left his friends alone and they ignored each other. All day.

'At least it's quiet,' Mark thought. But he knew that wasn't helping the band.

Mark did the shopping on his way home, so it was 4.30 by the time he got in. He pushed the kitchen door open – no screaming. The whole house was silent. It was peaceful – but a bit spooky.

There was a note from Janet on the kitchen table. It said –

I've taken Baby Amber for a walk. Back in time for tea. Mum's asleep. Don't wake her up!

So Mark unpacked the shopping, very quietly. Then he crept round the kitchen, grilling sausages and cooking broccoli and potatoes. By the time Janet got home from her walk, tea was on the table.

"You're a star, Mark!" Janet said. "And look!"

She pointed at the buggy. Baby Amber's face was red, as if she'd been crying – but she was fast asleep!

The smell of the sausages cooking woke Mum up and when she came downstairs there was a big, big smile on her face.

"Well done, you two!" she said. "I told you we could manage without Dad."

Mark grinned. "Too right we can," he said. "Everything's going to be fine."

But he was wrong – again.

Chapter 4
The Baby Rocker

The next morning, Mum woke up with a sore head and a runny nose. She looked *terrible*.

"I think I've got flu," she groaned. She felt far too ill to get out of bed.

"I'll stay at home and look after you," Janet said.

Mum shook her head. "You can't miss school," she croaked. "I'll manage somehow – just till you get back. And we'll be all right after that – it's Saturday tomorrow."

"I'll be here all day then," Janet said. "And Mark will help too, after his band practice. Right, Mark?"

"Right," Mark muttered.

There might not even be a practice on Saturday, but he wasn't going to tell Janet that. Things might be better by then. Maybe Jakob and Emma would be speaking when he got to school today.

They were speaking all right – but not to each other. They were using other people as messengers.

"Nell – please tell Jakob he's stupid," Emma kept saying.

Jakob pretended not to hear her. He spoke to Mark instead. "Tell Emma she's wrecked the band," he said.

They went on like that all day. Mark couldn't wait to leave school. Janet might have taken Baby Amber for another walk. It might be lovely and quiet at home.

But it wasn't. He heard Baby Amber screaming as soon as he opened the kitchen door. And there was another sound too.

Janet was crying.

Something awful must be wrong. Janet *never* cried. Not even the time she fell off her bike and broke her arm. Mark opened the door and ran in.

Baby Amber was on the floor in her baby rocker, screaming and screaming. And Janet was sitting at the table with her head in her hands, crying and crying.

"What's the matter?" Mark said.

"I don't know what to do," Janet sobbed. "I think I've got flu as well. I feel so *ill*."

She looked ill. She looked terrible.

"Go to bed," Mark said. "I'll look after the baby."

"You?" Janet sniffed and wiped her eyes. "But you don't know anything about babies. And you hate her screaming."

"I can manage," Mark said. "Just go to bed."

He thought Janet would refuse, but she didn't. That showed how ill she was. She stood up and tottered off to her bedroom, leaving Mark and Baby Amber alone together.

Mark took a deep breath. 'Here we go,' he thought.

He did everything he could think of to stop Baby Amber screaming. He changed her nappy

and bounced her in her rocker. He pulled funny
faces and wiggled his ears. He picked her up
and danced with her, rocking her in his arms.

But nothing was any good. She just screamed louder and *louder* and LOUDER.

At last, Mark couldn't think of anything else to do. He put Amber back in the baby rocker and strapped her in. Her face was bright red and she looked hot and angry.

"I'm sorry," Mark said, looking down at her. "You'll just have to go on screaming. I'm going to do some practice."

He took his guitar out of its case, turned his back on Baby Amber and started playing.

It was hard to focus because of the screaming, so he put on his headphones to shut out the noise. He closed his eyes and hummed, nodding in time to the music.

After a while, he noticed an odd kind of ... silence. 'Help!' he thought. 'Is the baby all right?' He turned round to look at her, still playing.

She wasn't screaming.

Chapter 5
The Magic of Music

Baby Amber was sitting in her rocker, staring up at Mark with her big dark blue eyes.

"Hey!" Mark said. "You like music, don't you?" He put the guitar down and took off his headphones.

But the moment he stopped playing, Baby Amber started screaming again, even louder than before. She screamed so hard her face scrunched up and she looked as if she was going to pop.

"OK, OK," Mark said, and he picked up his guitar again. "Here's some more music."

He started playing again – and straight away Baby Amber stopped screaming. She gazed up at him in wonder and he played and played, choosing his favourite songs and singing all the words.

He could have gone on for hours, but after a while he heard Mum calling in a wobbly voice.

"Mark!" she said. "I can't hear Baby Amber. Is she all right?"

Mark kept playing, very softly, as he went to the bottom of the stairs. "Amber's fine," he called up to Mum. "She's really happy."

"I need to feed her," Mum said. "Can you bring her up here, please?"

Mark carried Baby Amber upstairs. By the time he got to Mum's bedroom, she was screaming again, so he whispered in her ear. "It's OK, baby. I'll play the guitar again when you've had some milk."

He gave her to Mum and then went downstairs to make some sandwiches. After all that playing, he was *starving*. But he didn't care. He felt like a hero.

He'd discovered how to stop the baby crying.

There was only one problem ...

He couldn't play the guitar to Baby Amber all the time. He had lots of other things to do. Like making drinks for Mum and Janet. And changing Amber's nappy. And washing up. And every time he put his guitar down to do those things, Amber screamed and *screamed* and SCREAMED.

By the time it was dark, Mark's fingers were sore and his hands hurt from holding the guitar.

At 9.30, Mum called him upstairs. "Give the baby to me," she said. "You've been wonderful with her, but you need to go to bed now."

"If I stop playing she'll scream," Mark said.

"Then we'll have to let her scream," said Mum. "You can't stay awake playing the guitar all night. Off to bed!"

As Mark got into bed, he could hear Baby Amber screaming. 'She wants more music,' he thought. 'But I can't play all the time ... I can't ... if only ...'

Then – just as he was falling asleep – he had an idea. What about the *radio*?

'That's it!' he thought. 'That's the answer!' He nearly got out of bed and went to tell Mum, but he was too tired and soon his eyes were closing.

'I'll try the radio tomorrow,' he thought. 'Tomorrow ...'

Chapter 6

Help!

As soon as Mark woke up on Sunday morning, he jumped out of bed and ran into Mum's bedroom.

"Give me the baby!" he said.

Mum's face was grey and she kept yawning. "Poor Baby Amber's been screaming all night," she said. "I haven't had any sleep."

"Nor have I," Janet called from her bedroom. "PLEASE keep the baby quiet, Mark."

"Don't worry," Mark said with a grin. "I've worked out how to keep her happy."

He took Baby Amber downstairs and strapped her into her rocker. "Here you are," he said. "Here's some music for you!" And he turned on the radio.

But it didn't work.

Baby Amber stared at the radio for about ten seconds and then she started yelling, even louder than before. Mark tried changing the station. He went through all the stations, trying all kinds of different music. But it was no use. Baby Amber didn't like the radio. She didn't stop screaming until at last Mark picked up his guitar and started to play.

What else could he do? He was still in his pyjamas and he was very hungry. But if he stopped playing, Baby Amber would start screaming again. Then Mum and Janet would wake up.

Somehow or other he had to keep the baby quiet.

If only there was someone else who could play while he ate his breakfast. If only ...

That was when Mark had his second idea. And it was BRILLIANT.

He kept strumming the guitar with one hand. With the other hand, he took out his phone and texted Nell.

Come and practise at my house. Now. PLEASE!!!

Nell texted back.

Can't carry the drums. But I'll bring my tambourine and triangle!

'Good!' Mark thought. 'That's one band member on side.'

He kept strumming away and sent two more texts.

Hi Jakob. Fancy coming round to practise at my house this morning?

Hi Emma. How about coming round with your keyboard?

They both texted back straight away.

Great! said Jakob.

I'm on my way! said Emma.

Nell arrived first, with her triangle and tambourine, and Emma was right behind her, carrying the keyboard. Mark opened the front door – still playing his guitar – and they both grinned when they saw him.

"Love your pyjamas!" Emma said.

"Where's the baby?" said Nell. She ran past Mark, into the sitting room. When she saw Baby Amber, she kneeled down beside the rocker.

"Don't kiss her!" Mark almost shouted. "She doesn't like being kissed. The only thing she likes is music. If I stop playing, she screams."

"Let's see how she likes the keyboard," Emma said. She put it on the table and plugged in the lead. "Listen to this, Baby Amber," she said.

She started playing one of Vampire Jam's best songs and Nell picked up her triangle and joined in. Baby Amber stared up at Emma. Then at Nell. Then back at Emma. And she didn't scream. Not even when Mark put his guitar down.

"That's great," Mark said. "Keep playing while I go and take these daft pyjamas off."

But before Mark could do anything, the doorbell rang again. He opened the front door and there in front of him stood Jakob.

Chapter 7

Good Enough?

Jakob stood on the doorstep with a big smile on his face. Then he stepped inside and heard the keyboard – and his smile disappeared.

"Is that Emma?" Jakob said. "You didn't tell me *she* was coming."

Emma heard his voice. "Is that *Jakob*?" she screeched. "If he's here, I'm not staying!" She turned her keyboard off and unplugged it.

For a moment there was silence. Then Baby Amber opened her mouth and began to scream.

Emma went pale and Jakob put his hands over his ears.

"What's the matter?" Nell shouted. "What's wrong?"

"It's because the music stopped," Mark shouted back. "Quick! Start playing, everyone!"

"I'm not playing with Jakob!" Emma said.

"I'm not singing if Emma's here!" Jakob said.

They glared at each other.

Mark thought they were going to stomp out of the house. But then Baby Amber gave a huge, huge SCRE-E-E-EAM.

"*Please* just play!" Mark cried over the noise of Baby Amber. "Mum and Janet are ill. Please don't let her wake them up."

Emma ran back into the sitting room and plugged in her keyboard. And as soon as she started playing, Jakob began to sing.

Baby Amber stopped in the middle of a scream. She stared up at Jakob and Emma.

"Wow," Jakob said. "That's really cool. Your baby sister likes my singing!"

Mark started to play too and Nell picked up her triangle and joined in. Now all four of them were playing together. Baby Amber blinked and gazed around at them.

"She likes us," Emma whispered. "She's our very first fan."

Mark took a deep breath and put his guitar down. "Please keep playing while I get dressed," he whispered to the others. "Then I'll make us all some breakfast."

"Toast and jam for me, please," Nell whispered back. She jingled the tambourine.

"And me," said Emma.

She played a little run of notes on the keyboard and Jakob sang along with the tune she'd made up.

"Toast for me too," he sang. "With lots of marmalade."

Emma laughed and played a few more notes of her new tune. "Sing some more, Jakob," she said.

Jakob laughed. "But Amber wants music," he sang.

By the time Mark came back with a plateful of hot toast, Jakob and Emma had written a brand new song.

"Listen," said Nell. "Isn't this fantastic? Sing it again, Jakob."

Emma started playing her tune and Jakob sang the words he'd made up. He sang –

"Toast for me please.
With lots of marmalade.
But Amber wants music – music all day long
She's a cool, cooooooooooooooooool baby!
A real music-lover
And she's got great taste –
she loves our song!
It's better than toast and marmalade!"

The words were totally silly, but the tune was brilliant. Just listening to it made Mark smile.

"That's ace," he said. "Miles better than all our other songs." He looked at his friends. "I think it's good enough for the school show."

Jakob stopped smiling.

"Don't be silly, Jakob," Nell said. "You know it's a great song. It really is good enough for the show."

"We-ell ..." Jakob said.

"Let's do it," said Emma. "Please, Jakob."

"We'd have to practise a lot," Jakob said. "Once a week isn't enough."

"Fantastic!" said Mark. "Let's practise here – every day. Then we'll soon be good enough – and Amber won't scream any more."

Chapter 8
The Show

So that was what they did. The whole band came to Mark's house every day and they practised for an hour.

When Mark's dad came back from Ibiza, he thought they were wonderful.

"I can't wait for the show!" he said. "Granny's coming too – even if she has to walk on crutches. And she's bringing all her friends."

"We'd better practise harder!" Mark said.

So they practised for *two* hours every day –
before school and after school. Emma and
Jakob wrote some more verses for the song and
they played it over and over again, until they
were perfect. All the time they played, Baby
Amber listened happily. Not screaming at all.

The day before the show, Mum said, "We're
all coming to watch you play – Dad and I and
Janet and Granny and four of Granny's friends."

"But – what about Baby Amber?" Mark said.
"Who's looking after her?"

"She's coming too," Mum said. "Of course."

"No!" said Mark. "She'll scream all the
time."

"I don't think she will," said Mum. "Don't
worry."

But Mark did worry. Before the show
started, he peeped through the curtains and

saw them all in the very front row – Mum, Dad, Janet, Granny, Granny's friends ... and Baby Amber. If Baby Amber started screaming, she'd ruin the whole show.

The curtains opened and the Head Teacher walked onto the stage. "Welcome to our show!" she said. "There's a lot of talent in this school and I know you're going to enjoy the evening. So let's get going! Please welcome Vampire Jam!"

Everyone clapped as Mark and the rest of the band leaped onto the stage. The show was on!

As Mark played the opening riff on his guitar, Baby Amber's mouth opened.

'Oh *no*,' Mark thought. 'It's scream time again!'

But he was wrong. Baby Amber wasn't screaming. She was *smiling*. Her very first smile.

Jakob started singing. "Toast for me, please. And lots of marmalade," he sang.

And Amber's smile got bigger and bigger and bigger. She smiled all the way through their song – and then she fell asleep for the rest of the show.

At the end of the evening, everyone said their song was the best thing in the whole show. It was so catchy that Mark could hear people singing it as they walked out of the hall.

"That was a great song!" the Head Teacher said to Mark. "What's it called?"

"I – er –" Mark realised that he hadn't thought about a name.

But Nell had. "It's called *Amber's Song!*" she said.

GILLIAN CROSS has written lots of lively, funny stories including ...

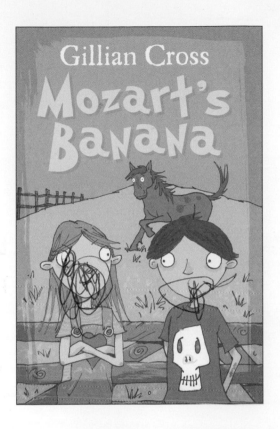

Mozart's Banana, a crazy name for a crazy horse.

No one can tame Mozart's Banana. Even Sammy Foster failed, and he reckons he's the boss of the school. Mozart's Banana is just too crazy.

But then Alice Brett turns up. Alice is as cool as a choc-ice, and she isn't going to let anyone get the better of her, horse or boy ...

www.barringtonstoke.co.uk